MEET ALL THESE FRIENDS IN BUZZ BOOKS:

Thomas the Tank Engine
The Animals of Farthing Wood
Fireman Sam
Looney Tunes
Bugs Bunny
Flintstones
Joshua Jones
Rupert

First published in Great Britain 1993
by Buzz Books
an imprint of Reed International Books Limited
Michelin House, 81 Fulham Road, London SW3 6RB
and Auckland, Melbourne, Singapore and Toronto

Rupert Characters™ & © 1993 Express Newspapers plc.
Licensed by Nelvana Marketing Inc.,
U.K. representatives: Abbey Home Entertainment Licensing
Text © copyright 1993 Methuen Children's Books
Illustrations © copyright 1993 Methuen Children's Books

ISBN 1 85591 283X

Printed in Italy by Olivotto

RUPERT
and the
DIZZY DONKEY

Story by Norman Redfern
Illustrations by SPJ Design

buzz books

"It's a perfect drying day!" said Mrs Bear to Rupert one morning. "The sun is out and there's a lovely fresh breeze!"

Rupert carried the basket of wet clothes into the garden, and watched as his mother hung them out to dry. The shirts flapped in the wind, as if they were eager to fly away.

"It would be fun to fly a kite on a day like this," said Rupert. "May I ask Willie Mouse if he'd like to take his kite out?"

"Of course you may," said Mrs Bear. She went into the larder and found two shiny red apples. "Here's one for you, and one for Willie, in case you feel hungry later."

Rupert knocked at his friend's front door.
Willie peeped timidly through the window.

"Oh, it's you, Rupert," he said, and he
opened the door.

"Hello, Willie," said Rupert, "I was
wondering if..."

Willie's whiskers fluttered in the breeze.
"I bet I know what you're going to ask!"
he said. "Come in while I put on my shoes.
Then we'll take my kite to the top of the hill
and see how high it will go!"

Willie Mouse was ready in a moment, and
together they set off across the common
and up the lane that led to the foot of the
hill. As they climbed the grassy slope,
Rupert remembered the two shiny red
apples. He had left them on Willie Mouse's
kitchen table.

At the top of the hill, Willie unrolled the ball of string and ran through the grass with the box kite behind him. Suddenly, a gust of wind caught the kite and tried to pull it away from the little mouse.

"Help!" cried Willie. "If I let go of the string, I'll never see my kite again!"

"Hold on tight, Willie!" called Rupert.

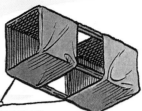

The string raced through Willie's fingers as the kite flew higher and higher.

Rupert ran to Willie's side and gripped the string with all his might, but then another fierce gust of wind tugged the string so hard that even Rupert had to let go.

"Look!" cried Rupert, as the kite sailed away. "It's going to catch in that tree!"

Rupert and Willie raced to the tall oak tree which had caught the kite in its branches.

"It's a very tall tree," said Willie nervously.

"Don't worry, Willie," said Rupert. "I'll bring your kite down."

Rupert climbed the oak tree carefully, holding its sturdy branches tightly, until he was level with the kite.

"I can't reach from here," he told Willie.
"I shall have to crawl along this branch."
Willie watched as Rupert edged his way
nearer to the kite.

"I've got the kite!" Rupert called down to his friend as he clutched the string. "What a view! I can see everything from up here. There's Nutwood, and there's Popton, and — wait a minute, that's funny — "

"What is it?" asked Willie, but Rupert was already on his way back down.

He handed Willie his kite and told him what he had seen from the treetop.

"There's a donkey in the farmer's field down the lane," he said, "and it looked as if it was dancing! Since the wind is much too strong for kite flying, shall we go and see what's the matter with the donkey?"

The little bear eagerly led his friend back
down the hill.

"Listen," he said. From the other side of
the hedge there came an angry bellow.
A few yards further on, they found a stile.
Rupert was about to climb over when
suddenly he heard the thunder of hooves,
and there stood the donkey.

16

"It doesn't look very friendly," said Willie.

"No, and here's why," replied Rupert. "The poor donkey has an old bag of rubbish caught on his ear. I expect it was left behind by picnickers from the city. Every time he shakes his head, the bag flaps about. No wonder he's feeling dizzy!"

Rupert reached carefully towards the carrier bag.

"I must try to lift it off his ear without hurting him," he told Willie. But as he leaned over the stile, the donkey took fright and started shaking its head even more anxiously.

"He won't let me near enough to help him," said Rupert. "We must find a way to calm him down." Rupert thought for a moment. "I know! Willie, will you please run back to Nutwood and ask the Chinese Conjurer if he has any spells for charming angry beasts?"

Rupert waited by the stile as the little
mouse skipped down the lane. He hoped
that Willie would be back soon.

"Don't worry," he told the donkey.
"We'll help you take off that horrible bag.
Just wait a little bit longer, please."

20

It seemed to be a very long wait. Rupert tried to stroke the donkey's back, but every time he reached his hand across the stile, the frightened creature jumped away.

Then, from along the lane, he heard Willie Mouse talking to someone. It must be the Chinese Conjurer!

"Rupert!" called Willie. "The Conjurer was out, but I've brought Tigerlily instead."

"Hello Rupert," said the Conjurer's daughter, "I hear you need some magic!"

"It's this poor donkey," said Rupert. "He must be charmed into lying down so that I can take that nasty bag off his ear."

"I know just the spell!" said Tigerlily.

Rupert was worried. What if Tigerlily's spell went wrong? Then he had an idea.

"We don't need a spell, Tigerlily," he replied. "Just sing the donkey the sweetest lullaby you know."

Tigerlily understood at once, and began singing quietly. When the donkey heard the beautiful old Chinese melody, it stopped jumping and listened, its head tilted to one side. Slowly, it lay down in the long grass, closed its big brown eyes, and fell asleep.

"Thank you, Tigerlily," said Rupert.

He climbed over the stile and carefully slid the bag's handles off the donkey's ear.

"We must put that in a litter bin where it won't harm any other creatures," he said, passing the bag across the stile to Willie.

"Look out, Rupert!" cried Willie.

Rupert turned round to see the donkey, wide awake again, strolling towards him.

"Hello, Donkey," he said. "That bag won't hurt you any more."

The donkey moved its head up and down, as if it were nodding to Rupert. Then it gently butted him, walked a few steps away, and waited.

"He wants me to follow him!" said Rupert.

"Be careful," warned Willie Mouse.

Willie and Tigerlily watched the donkey
lead Rupert through a gap in the hedge and
into another field. Then they heard a
strange noise. It sounded as if the donkey
was butting something rather hard.

"Oh, no! What's happened?" cried Willie.

Rupert walked back through the gap in the hedge. The donkey trotted happily behind him.

"He wants to say thank you," said Rupert.

"But what was that awful sound?" Willie asked his friend.

"Oh, he was just helping the wind to shake the trees in that orchard," replied Rupert, bringing his hands out from behind his back. There, in his open palms, were three ripe, shiny, red apples to munch on the way home to Nutwood.